Lovey Dove Flies West

CARLENE BROD

To order additional copies of this book, contact:
Xlibris
844-714-8691
www.Xlibris.com
Orders@Xlibris.com

ISBN: Softcover   978-1-6698-7857-5
           EBook   978-1-6698-7856-8

Print information available on the last page

Rev. date: 05/22/2023

Lovey Dove Flies West

DEDICATIONS

THANKS TO THE CONTRIBUTIONS FROM:

- ❖ BRUCE BROD MD
- ❖ MADISON BROD PHD
- ❖ MARCIA BROD
- ❖ ROY BROD MD
- ❖ DAVID MILLER

Hello Love Dove

Lovey Dove is flying to the western United States.
Lovey is leaving from Boathouse Row in Philadelphia.
There are many boat races on the Schuylkill River.

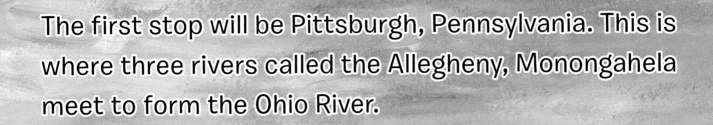

The first stop will be Pittsburgh, Pennsylvania. This is where three rivers called the Allegheny, Monongahela meet to form the Ohio River.

In Chicago, Illinois there is a very large sculpture known as the Bean. It allows visitors to go underneath and see their reflection.

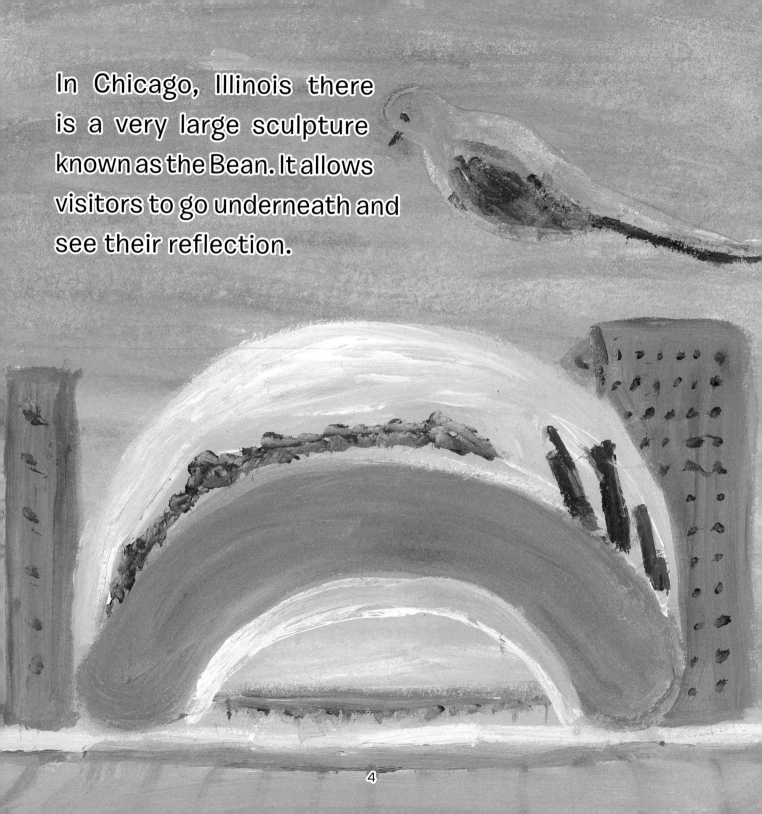

St. Louis, Missouri is home to the tallest man made monument in the United States called the Gateway Arch. It is very tall and known as the Gateway to the West.

Kansas is called the Sunflower State. Lovey will stop here among the beautiful flowers.

Colorado is one of the four corner states. They are Arizona, Colorado, Nevada and Utah. Lovey will stop on the meeting spot.

Hot air balloons are a famous sight in New Mexico. Lovey will try to fly as high as they are.

In Arizona, the beautiful Grand Canyon was carved from the Colorado River. Lovey will stop on one of the hiking trails.

There are many opportunities for fun in Utah such as biking, hiking, skiing and camping.

Yellowstone National Park occupies space in Wyoming, Idaho and Montana. It is famous for Geysers that erupt hot water from the ground.

Nevada has many cactus plants due to the hot, dry climate. Lovey will stop to see them.

Muir Woods in California is the next stop. The tall redwood trees are more than 150 years old.

Lovey's visit to the Golden Gate Bridge in California is a special experience. The water under the bridge connects the Pacific Ocean with the San Francisco Bay.

San Diego Zoo is the last stop for Lovey. The Safari Park is a special part of the zoo. The zoo is a leader in conserving wildfire.

Lovey Dove had a wonderful trip across the United States from East to West.

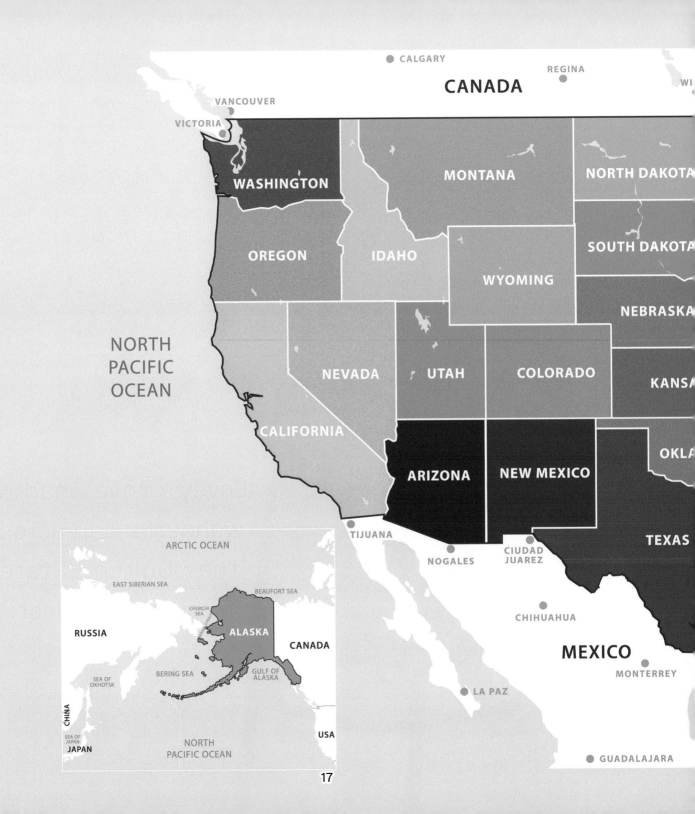

NORTH
PACIFIC
OCEAN

CALGARY

REGINA

WI

CANADA

VANCOUVER

VICTORIA

WASHINGTON

MONTANA

NORTH DAKOTA

OREGON

IDAHO

SOUTH DAKOTA

WYOMING

NEBRASKA

NEVADA

UTAH

COLORADO

KANSAS

CALIFORNIA

ARIZONA

NEW MEXICO

OKLA

TEXAS

TIJUANA

NOGALES

CIUDAD
JUAREZ

CHIHUAHUA

MEXICO

MONTERREY

LA PAZ

GUADALAJARA

ARCTIC OCEAN

EAST SIBERIAN SEA

BEAUFORT SEA

CHUKCHI
SEA

RUSSIA

ALASKA

CANADA

SEA OF
OKHOTSK

BERING SEA

GULF OF
ALASKA

CHINA

USA

SEA OF
JAPAN

JAPAN

NORTH
PACIFIC OCEAN

17

United States
of America

QUEBEC

OTTAWA   MONTREAL

MAINE

Lake Superior

Lake Huron

WISCONSIN

Lake Michigan

TORONTO
Lake Ontario

VT

NH

MICHIGAN

Lake Erie

NEW YORK

MA

CT RI

...OTA

...OWA

ILLINOIS   IN   OHIO

PENNSYLVANIA

NJ

MISSOURI

WEST
VIRGINIA

MD

Washington
D.C.

DE

KENTUCKY

VIRGINIA

CT = CONNECTICUT
D.C. = DISTRICT OF COLUMBIA
DE = DELAWARE
FL = FLORIDA
IN = INDIANA
MA = MASSACHUSETTS
MD = MARYLAND
MS = MISSISSIPPI
NH = NEW HAMPSHIRE
NJ = NEW JERSEY
RI = RHODE ISLAND
VT = VERMONT

...ARKANSAS

TENNESSEE

NORTH
CAROLINA

SOUTH
CAROLINA

NORTH ATLANTIC OCEAN

MS   ALABAMA   GEORGIA

LOUISIANA

HAWAIIAN ISLANDS

HAWAÏ

NORTH
PACIFIC
OCEAN

USA

MEXICO

FLORIDA

GULF OF MEXICO

★ NASSAU

BAHAMAS

★ LA HAVANE

MERIDA

CANCÙN

CUBA

18

Printed in the United States
by Baker & Taylor Publisher Services